Jack and the Beanstalk

Ian Beck

OXFORD

UNIVERSITY PRESS

Once upon a time, in the age of magic, there was a boy called Jack. He lived with his mother in a little house on their farm. They were very poor, and the only possession they had left was Daisy the cow. Daisy was a very nice, but very old, cow and was the only real friend that Jack had.

But one day Jack's mother decided he must take Daisy to market and sell her or else they would starve.

The next morning Jack set off with Daisy, to walk to market. His mother waved them goodbye. 'Make sure you get a good price!' she said.

Jack was sad to be selling Daisy, so he walked very slowly, hoping to be too late for the market.

After a while they met an old man. He looked very odd. He was bent almost double and wore strange clothes, all coloured green.

'Good morning, boy,' said the old man.
'What a fine cow. Where are you taking her?'

'I must take her to market and sell her,
for we are very poor,' said Jack with a sigh.

'I never saw such a splendid animal,'
said the old man. 'I should like to buy her
myself.' And with that he took out five beans
from his purse.

Jack had hoped for some gold coins. 'I
couldn't sell Daisy for beans,' he said.

'Ah,' said the old man, 'but these are magic
beans. Plant them in your garden by moonlight
and you will see.'

When Jack got home, his mother called him a fool. It was worse than she had feared, she said. Now they really would starve.

But Jack believed the old man, and that night, under the full moon, he planted the five beans.

His mother woke him early. 'Now look what you've done!' she cried.

Jack hopped out of bed, and into the garden. Those beans really had been magic. Where he had planted them there now stood an enormous beanstalk. It stretched up into the sky and beyond the clouds.

Jack saw at once a chance for adventure and perhaps even a fortune. Straightaway he began to climb.

Up

and up

he went,

higher

and

higher,

until he found himself above the clouds and in a different world.

Ahead of him stretched a long twisty road and at the end of the road stood a huge castle.

Jack walked up to the castle and climbed
the steep steps to the door.

'Whoever lives here must be a giant,' said
Jack. He slipped into the castle through a
crack in the door and came into a vast room
with a fire blazing.

By the table was a wooden cage and in the
cage Jack could see a fat white goose tied by
a rope.

'Honk! Help me escape from here,' said the goose, 'and you will never be poor again, for I am a magic goose.'

Now Jack had good reason to believe in magic; the old man had been right about the beans after all. 'All right,' said Jack. 'I'll have you out of there in no time.'

But as he started to pull on the bars there came a sound like thunder,

BOOM . . . BOOM . . . BOOM,

and with it a voice low and loud . . .

'Fee, Fi, Fo, Fum
I smell the blood
of an Englishman
Be he alive or be he dead
I'll grind his bones
to make my bread.'

'Quick,' said the goose, 'it's the giant! Hide!' So Jack climbed onto the table and hid behind a huge egg-cup.

The door crashed open and in walked the giant. He sat at the table, banged down his great fist, and laughed, 'Ho, ho, ho … where is my lovely goosey-goosey?'

The giant picked up the cage and the goose. He pulled open the door, sat the poor goose down in the middle of the table, and boomed out, 'Lay, goose, lay.' The goose let out a sad 'honk', and laid an egg.

The giant picked up the egg and laughed again, 'Ho, ho, ho,' and then carefully put the egg in the egg-cup. It was an egg of solid gold. Jack stared – it really was a magic goose. 'Lay, goose, lay,' said the giant again, and again the goose laid a golden egg, and so on until it had laid six eggs in all. Jack watched as the giant fell asleep with a big smile on his face.

Jack crept out from behind the egg-cup and quickly untied the rope from the goose's neck. 'Climb onto my back,' said the goose.

And with Jack on her back she flew up and out of the castle window.

The flap of her wings woke the giant, and as they flew down the road towards the beanstalk, he blundered after them. 'Come back!' he shouted.

Jack hurled himself down the beanstalk, while the goose flew down beside him. But the giant started to climb down the beanstalk as well.

Jack saw his mother at the bottom of the beanstalk and he called to her to fetch the axe. As soon as Jack reached the ground he took the axe and chopped until the beanstalk and the giant crashed to the ground.

The giant, being so heavy, made such a hole that he fell right through the earth and was never seen again.

When Jack's mother saw the huge goose she was cross. 'Whatever is that ugly bird?' she said. 'We can hardly feed ourselves, let alone a thing like that.'

'It's a magic goose,' said Jack. 'Watch this. Lay, goose, lay,' he said to the goose, and patted it kindly on the head.

The goose let out a happy 'honk' and laid a single golden egg, as it did once a year every year from then on.

And so Jack, and his mother, and the goose, lived happily in comfort for the rest of their days.

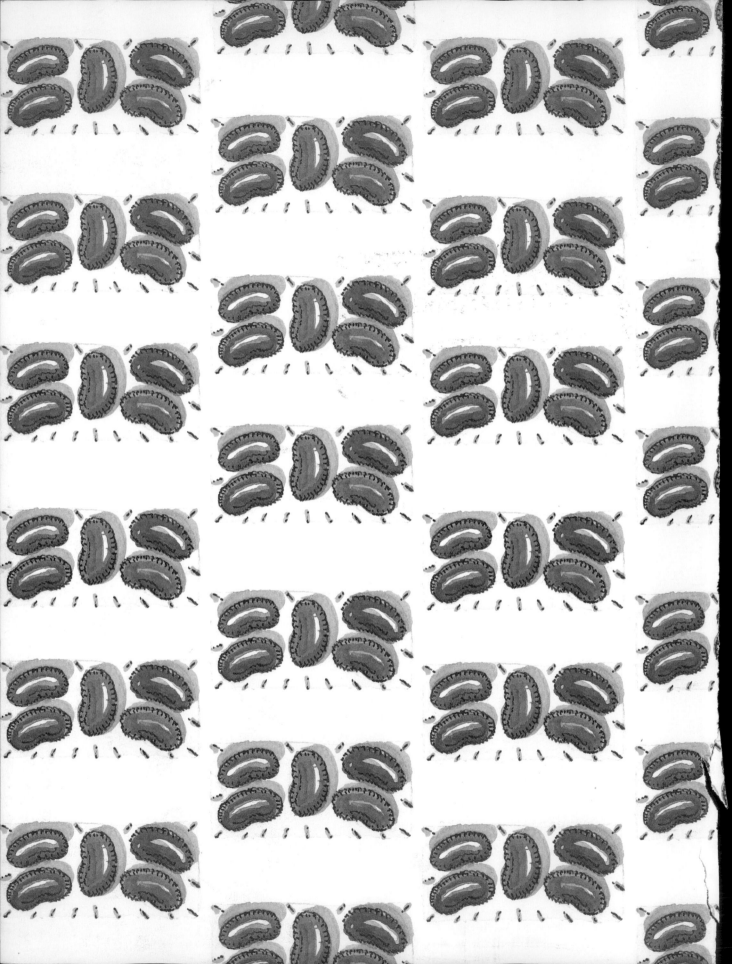